Anna Claus

The Woman Behind The Legend

Jolene Giordano and Linda Dockery

Best Wishes

Linda Dockery

Anna Claus
The Woman Behind The Legend
Copyright [C] 2003 Dockery & Giordano

ISBN: 0-9700344-4-X

Printed in the United States of America

Angel Publishing paperbacks edition 2003

Dedicated To:

**Everyone Who Still Believes in the
Magic of Christmas**

A Very Special Thank You to <u>Ann Koch</u>

Anna Claus

The Woman Behind the Legend

Everyone knows my husband; he's one of the most recognized men in the world. Children adore him, and dream of his flight on that cold December night. Books are written about him, movies made about his life, and poems honor his name. But no one knows him the way I do for you see; I am Mrs. Santa Claus.

Anna Claus is such a wonderful story about a woman we know so little about.
It will be treasured by young and old alike.

John Vetch
Christian Booksellers

A wonderful story that finally reveals the reclusive Anna Claus to the world.

Mike Decker
Author / Teacher

So visual, so realistic. I felt like I was there.

Jane Willoughby
Barnes & Noble Booksellers

Reading Anna Claus made me remember many wonderful memories from my youth, and how special Christmas it to all children.

Allison Bateman
Author

It made me wish I were a child again.

Pat Minton
Bantams Booksellers

Anna Claus

The Woman Behind The Legend

When first approached to do this interview, I thought my editor had finally slipped off the deep end. I wondered if she had spent so much time, elbow deep in manuscripts of fiction, that her concept of reality had been damaged. I politely declined her offer, fearful of upsetting her while she was in such a fragile state of mind, yet she persisted. I tried explaining that I had stopped believing in Santa when I was eight years old and a trip to the North Pole was simply out of the question for I had already packed away my winter clothing. Still she persisted.

The more I listened to her explain how she had received a phone call directly from Mrs. Claus, the more certain I became that men in white coats were waiting outside her office to carry her away. When I questioned as to why she had selected me over all the writers available, she informed me that it was because of my strong disbelief in Santa and all the holiday trappings that went along with his image. Because of my belief's, she assumed that I would be more objective. And the fact that I was the only one available had a little to do with it.

Deciding it may be best to play along with her fantasy, so not to make her more delusional than she already was; I finally relented and accepted the assignment. As she handed me the plane ticket and travel instructions, I figured, 'what the heck,' a vacation might be nice. Besides, I always had an adventurous nature and a curiosity for the unknown, so this trip might be rather interesting. Who knows? Maybe I might discover some fresh material for my next book.

As she ushered me to the door, my agent, [who was now exuberant that I had accepted the assignment,] attempted to offer instructions on how to behave around the woman who was married to the most beloved man in the world. As she opened the door and escorted me into the hall, I glanced both ways, expecting to hear someone jump out and shout, "Smile, you're on Candid Camera."

The entire trip down the elevator, and even out onto the street where I hailed a cab, my agent continued chattering like an excited chipmunk. I couldn't believe the woman, whom I normally considered a very rational person, was acting like a schoolchild. As I anxiously climbed into the cab, I found myself relieved to get away from her before her oncoming insanity rubbed off on me. Not until then did I take time to examine the papers she had shoved into my hands. Sure enough, the plane ticket stated Canada.

As I watched the city of New York whiz past my cab window, I had no idea what was waiting me. I figured it would be a brief jaunt across the border to pacify my insane editor. I had never been to Canada and it sounded appealing since I already had a free plane ticket. Little did I know that I was embarking on the adventure of my life.

The first leg of my trip was uneventful. When the plane landed in Toronto, I gathered my luggage and waited to be contacted, as were my instructions. I had only enough time to inhale a cold deli sandwich of what I hoped was tuna salad, and then wash it down with a glass of cola before I was approached by an older gentleman in his mid-fifties. He handed me a letter of introduction and promptly gathered my luggage. With a nod of his head motioned for me to follow. The letter also stated that he would be flying me to a place called Victoria Island.

"Sure, why not?" I thought to myself as I followed him through the busy terminal. One step deeper into my adventure, I climbed into his aircraft and fastened my seat belt. By now I had donned a heavy winter parka with a fur lined hood, gloves and ear muffs, all of which I would need as I glanced out the window to see the snow covered ground below

Passing over a large heard of caribou, I smiled as they raced away, fearful of the sound overhead. I chuckled softly at myself, wondering which one was Dasher, or Dancer. Maybe even Rudolph was in there someplace.

No sooner had the plane landed and I stepped out to stretch my legs, than another man approached with instructions. I was to fly with him to a location that only he knew, and there I was to wait until contacted by a man called Max. So the plot thickens. I was already neck deep into my adventure so I decided to play the hand out to the end. I had no idea where I was, only that I was surrounded by snow and ice and it was so cold I could see my breath freezing as it rushed from my nose and mouth.

At this point, I started to question the wisdom of allowing my editor to talk me into this. No one I spoke with would tell me anything. It felt like some covert operation that I was being led blindly into. My writer's imagination was running rampant; I had already come up with several scenarios as to what might lay ahead. One thing was certain; I had enough ideas to fill ten books when I returned home.

The ride in the helicopter was a bit unnerving as I had never been inside one before. It was one of those clear, bubble types where you can see everything around you. If you look down, you can see the earth moving past beneath your feet. It was quite an exhilarating experience. It also made me a little dizzy and that tuna salad sandwich was talking to me.

When the chopper finally landed, my first assumption was that the pilot had made a horrendous mistake, for there was nothing to see for miles except snow and a tiny one room log cabin. When I discovered that I was to wait there alone for Max to arrive, I began to get apprehensive. If I had not been wearing thick mittens, I might have chewed off my nails within a matter of moments. I could hear my nervous heart thumping in my ears. Maybe I had bitten off a bit too much with this adventure. I had allowed myself to be escorted to the top of the world by a man I had never seen before, and may never see again as I watched him climb back into the chopper.

Like a brave little trooper, I held my head high and marched into the cabin, dragging my luggage with me. From the window, I watched the giant blades stir up the fresh fallen snow as the helicopter rose and quickly disappeared into the horizon.

Instantly the silence closed in around me, it was deafening. Nothing stirred except an occasional swirl of snow caught on an Arctic wind. I looked out the tiny window at the frozen world around me. There was nothing but white as far as I could see. It was an extremely eerie feeling. I found myself singing Christmas tunes to occupy the time and to quiet the humming in my ears. Glancing around the tiny room, I was thrilled to see a welcoming fire blazing in the hearth, and a hot pot of coffee waiting on the old cast iron stove. Never once did it dawn on me to question who had started the fire, or made the coffee. With a full cup, I returned to the window to gaze out into the bleak whiteness of the Arctic Circle, wondering what fate had in store for me.

It seemed an eternity, and I believe I dozed off in the old rocking chair, before the distinct sound of someone crushing snow beneath their feet brought me back to reality. I stood quickly as the door opened and the smallest man I had ever seen appeared in the doorway. His smile seemed to reach from pointed ear to pointed ear, and a thick patch of beard covered his chin. His big brown eyes reminded me of rich chocolate and held a hint of elfin mischief. When he spoke, his voice rang out like chimes and I found serenity within it. I felt complete trust for this little man whom I had just laid eyes on for the first time. He felt like a warm, comfortable friend.

With his help, we packed my luggage onto a red sleigh being drawn by two large reindeer. I couldn't help but notice how their black leather harness glistened in the sunlight, and the bells that adorning them were polished to perfection. Nestled in the back seat beneath a thick blanket of fur, I watched as Max lifted the reins and the deer stepped lively into motion. With great ease the sleigh glided across the packed snow with little or no effort. Max handled the animals expertly, never bothering to glance back to see if I was still with him.

As we rode along, I found myself being drawn to the rainbow of colors that lit up the northern sky. The Aurora Borealis, or Northern Lights, put on a show worth any price of admission. I was transfixed by the wonder of it all and found myself unable to remove my stare from the glorious show Mother Nature was displaying for me.

It seemed we drove for an eternity and much to my surprise, I drifted off to sleep. Although I'm sure I dozed for only a moment, the sleigh bouncing on a bump brought me back to my senses. As my eyes adjusted, I found that we had literally driven into the Northern Lights, their beauty and wonder engulfing us, surrounding us with a blissfulness I had never known before. Fully alert, I sat upright and watched over Max's shoulder at the odd arrangements of lights that appeared in the distance. The closer we drew, the more I began to see that the lights were illuminating from the windows of homes and various buildings within the community.

To say I was wonder-struck would have been an understatement. Were my eyes deceiving me? Was I delusional from so long a time in the blinding snow? Surely the sight before me was some apparition that had appeared to confuse me even further. I knew that what I was seeing could not be real, yet there it was in all its wondrous glory.

The large red and white striped pole stuck out of the snow like a beacon and held a banner stating the words, 'North Pole.' The lane in which we traveled was lined with gingerbread houses trimmed with candy canes and lolly pops. It was a child's wildest fantasy comes true. No matter how I tried to find some logical explanation to what my eyes were showing me, the more I had to conclude that it was actually very real.

As the sled glided along, I watched with wonder as what appeared to be elves, scurried about attending to their duties. I felt a rush of excitement that surged clear down to my toes. I pinched myself to make certain that I was not dreaming, and the pain assured me that I was fully awake.

When Max drew the sleigh to a smooth stop before a magnificent log home, the likes of which I had never before seen, I gingerly stepped out onto the packed snow and followed him up onto the porch. My heart raced with such speed I felt it would surely burst within my chest. Was I actually standing at the door of Saint Nick's home? What would I say if he actually appeared to greet me? For someone who had stopped believing in Santa Claus many years before, this was a bit too much reality to handle at one time.

As Max started to reach for the knob, the massive door opened and there appeared the lady of my quest. Mrs. Claus stood before me with a smile that could warm the coldest of hearts. She was exactly as I imagined her to be. Plump in size, yet stately in stature. Her rosy-red cheeks matched in color the bright red sweater and skirt she wore, each decorated around the hem with white fur. A traditional Santa hat rested atop her head, partly covering her beautiful gray hair. But it was her eyes that held me transfixed for they were bright green and sparkled like two emeralds.

"For heaven's sake, come in before you catch your death of cold," she instructed in a musical voice that instantly make me feel welcome.

Without hesitation, I followed her into a large sitting room where a roaring fire blazed in a huge fireplace that adorned one wall. As she took my coat, I found myself studying every inch of the room, still unable to believe what my eyes stated to be true. A gloriously decorated Christmas tree stood in one corner of the room reaching from floor to ceiling. Strings of popcorn and red berries were woven through the limbs where hand made ornaments hung from each branch. Twinkling lights added to the festive mood of the room which was decorated in every nook and cranny with the spirit of Christmas. It was absolutely breath-taking in its grandeur.

"Maxwell, see to Mrs. Marr's luggage," Mrs. Clause instructed, and dismissed him with a wave of her hand. Turning her attention back to me, she smiled with grandmotherly affection. "I'm so thrilled you decided to come," she said with sincerity. "I hope you enjoy your visit, and if you need anything, just ask."

It took a moment to find my voice as I was still a bit overwhelmed by the entire ordeal. "I can't believe I'm actually here. When my editor asked me to take this assignment, I thought she was crazy. I have to be honest with you, I stopped believing in Santa a long time ago."

She let out a soft sigh, but not one of annoyance, one more of sadness. "I'm afraid that happens to most children as they grow older," she said with remorse. "Everyone here at toy land has tried to figure out what makes children stop believing. Maybe you can explain it to us."

As she looked to me for the answer, I had to shrug my shoulders for I really had no explanation to offer. All I could do was make an educated guess. "For me, I guess it came with the knowledge of discovering that it was actually my parents who bought the presents. I waited up one night with the hope of catching Santa in the act, and I saw my father placing packages around the tree."

"I guess it happens that way for many children," she accepted the explanation with another soft sigh. Quickly changing the subject, her face lit up and she again smiled. "You must be starved my dear." She took my arm and ushered me down a long hall to the massive kitchen.

I said not a word as I watched her rummage through one of the many cabinets to retrieve a bowl which she proceeded to fill with soup from the stove. Once I smelled the delicious aroma, I had to admit that a warm meal would be most welcomed.

"I know you must have a million questions to ask, but we can attend to than later," she instructed me. "First you eat, then you can retire to your room and rest. The trip must have been straining for you, my dear. I'll send someone in to assist you."

She started to leave the room, but stopped abruptly at the doorway and turned back to face me. "Dear me, in all the excitement of having you visit, I'm afraid I forgot my manners and did not properly introduce myself." Stepping back to the table, she extended her hand for me to accept. "I am Mrs. Santa Claus, but you may call me Anna."

"Anna," I smiled as her name rolled off my lips. "I'm Karen Marr." A slight chuckle escaped me as I again met her warm green eyes. "I still can't believe I'm really here."

"Yes, I imagine this is quite a shock for you." She patted my hand in a motherly fashion and flashed me a tender smile. "I'll give you time to adjust before I expose you to all the wonders of Toy Land. I must admit that it can be very overwhelming at first."

Before I could utter another word, she disappeared from the room amid a swish of her skirt and the jingle of the bells that adorned it. I was left alone with my thoughts, which at the moment were racing through my mind at an alarming rate.

The chicken soup, which was the most delicious I had ever known, warmed my insides and made me feel sleepy and content. As I ate the wondrous meal, I studied every inch of the huge kitchen with it four fireplaces, each one adorned with various pots, pans and utensils used for cooking and baking. Several extremely long tables filled one section of the room with a place setting laid out in front of each chair. This was, no doubt, where all the elves dined.

Hearing the door open, I watched as a female elf entered, her long golden hair cascading down her back like spun gold. "Mrs. Claus sent me to see to your needs. My name is Penny," she informed me in a soft, childlike voice. "If you are finished, I will escort you to your room."

As though in a trance, I stood and followed obediently as Penny led me through a maze of long halls, attempting to explain various rooms in which we passed along the way. The whole experience was still quite overwhelming, especially for someone like me who was positive that Santa was a myth created for the delight of childish fantasy. Yet, here I was in his home, being taken to my room by an elf called Penny. Will the wonders ever cease?

The bedroom, to which I was shown, was a child's dream come true. Toys were everywhere, lining the walls and overflowing from large toy boxes. Of all the room held, my eyes focused on the large sleigh bed with its thick feather mattress fluffed high and inviting.

"If you require anything, please ring the bell rope beside the bed," Penny informed me as she moved toward the door. "Mrs. Claus said you should get some rest after such a long trip. I will return for you this evening."

I was already crawling into the depths of the feather bed before the door had time to close behind her. The flannel sheets were warm and soothing to the touch as I nestled down for some much needed rest. With the comforter drawn securely to my neck, I closed my eyes and drifted off to sleep where I dreamed of candy canes, magical reindeer and Christmas's long since past.

****

I awoke to the delicious aroma of fresh brewed coffee and homemade Danish. Standing beside my bed, Mrs. Claus herself held a tray containing the objects of the enticing smells. "Thought you might like these," she said as she placed the tray across my lap. "I know they're your favorite."

Leaning back against the headboard, I sipped on the coffee, my eyes never leaving the woman who drew up a chair beside me and planted herself within it. "I thought Penny was coming after me," I stated, positive that was what the elf had stated.

"Oh she was about to," Anna assured me, " but I sent her to attend to other duties. I thought this would give us an opportunity to chat privately for a moment. I imagine you must have a million questions you want to ask."

"A million would be a low estimate," I lightheartedly returned, although I was unsure just how far from the truth it really was. "I was positive that when I awoke from my nap, I would be back in my New York apartment and this had all been a dream."

I looked around the room, still not certain if my agent's insanity had not rubbed off on me as well. "You must admit, this is unusual to say the least. To grasp the notion that I am actually having coffee in bed at the North Pole, served by Mrs. Clause herself, is a bit much for a skeptic like myself to easily accept."

Giving her chin a thoughtful scratch, she smiled as her eyes twinkled with acceptance. "I can understand what you're saying. If the roles were reversed, I would probably feel the same way being thrust into a situation that I didn't believe existed."

Sipping on the coffee, I noticed the distinctive taste of nutmeg. It pleased my pallet and I smiled with pleasure as the warm liquid slid down my throat. "This is delicious. I've never had coffee that tasted quite like this before."

A smile beamed on Anna's face, obviously pleased that I approved of the brew. "It's a favorite here at Toy Land," she informed me. "I was hoping you might like it."

My eyes opened wider in sheer delight as I bit into the Danish. It was like a taste of heaven, so light and creamy. The taste buds in my mouth were screaming for joy as I took yet another bite until it was consumed. "Never have I tasted anything so scrumptious," I said while attempting to wipe my lips on the napkin. "Keep this up and you'll spoil me shamelessly."

Anna beamed with pride at yet another compliment. It was easy to see that she was very pleased by my approval of the delicacies she provided. "My dear, I could show you items made in the kitchen that would make the great chef's in the world green with envy. Our elf chef's have recipes as old as time itself, each one a culinary treasure."

I could already feel my mouth watering just listening to her tell of mountain high cakes, piled with fluffy frosting. Cookies holding more chocolate chips that you could count, and evening meals that made me hungry just hearing their names. "You should write a cookbook," I suggested with sincerity. "Call it, ' Recipes from the North Pole.'

A twinkle came again to her eyes as she flashed me a surprised grin. "Funny you should say that, my dear. The elves and I have been working on such a book."

"I guess great minds think alike," I stated with a chuckle. Sitting the breakfast tray aside, I swung my legs over the side of the bed and stood. "I should get dressed so we can start our interview." I looked around for my clothing, but it was not draped over the chair as I had left it the previous night. Even my luggage was not to be seen. "Where are my things?" I asked curiously.

With a smile, Anna stood beside me and gently patted my hand. "Don't worry child, your things are safe. Penny came in after you fell asleep and hung your belongings in the closet." As she moved toward the door, she spoke without looking back. "Dress now and I'll have Penny fetch you shortly."

With that, she was gone. As I removed a pair of jeans and sweatshirt from the closet, I again wondered at my sanity. I studied every inch of the glorious room, even pinched myself again to make certain I was awake. . . I was.

"If this is real, then this will be the interview of a lifetime," I mumbled to myself as the actuality of what I was doing sank in to my mind. "I am about to interview the wife of Santa Clause, the Queen of the Frozen north, Anna Clause herself." I chuckled softly and felt my heart flutter within my chest. "I am actually at the North Pole, in Toy Land, and I may see the big man himself." By now my adrenaline was pumping at an alarming rate and I couldn't wait to get started.

Quickly snatching a camera, and small tape recorder from my briefcase, I headed for the door. Just as I was about to grasp the knob, the massive oak door opened to reveal Penny. "I came to retrieve you as Mrs. Clause instructed," she informed me with a motion of her hand to follow.

Without hesitation, I immediately fell into step behind her. My eyes darted from one extraordinary sight to the next, each one filling me with fascination. Massive rooms filled with toys from floor to ceiling, and elves scurrying about, attending to his, or her task. It was a wonderland of color and activity and I soon found myself becoming caught up in the excitement that filled the air. Arriving at our destination, we entered a small sitting room where I saw Anna seated in a rocker beside the hearth. Penny left me at the door and departed, closing it behind her. I studied the room and found it quaint and inviting, the kind of room that did honor to the lady who held court within it. The only Christmas decoration in sight was a cast iron miniature of a sleigh pulled by two reindeer with Santa in the driver's seat. It sat on the floor before the hearth. The wall over the hearth was filled with photos of elves, reindeer and just common people like myself. A sofa and two rockers sat in arrangement around the hearth for conversation and a window bench adorned the wall beside the large pane of glass that opened the room to a breathtaking view of the frozen world outside.

"Come, seat yourself by the fire," Anna suggested as she continued to stroke the black and white kitten curled up within the folds of her lap. "This is Kitty Girl," she introduced me to her companion. "Her brother, Kitty Boy, is wandering around someplace. Probably in the kitchen, that's his favorite haunt."

As I seated myself, the kitten gave me but a brief glance of acknowledgement before returning to the land of slumber. "Your home is fascinating," I found myself babbling. "Never in my wildest dreams did I imagine it to look anything like this."

"I love it here, and can't imagine living anyplace else," Anna confessed. "I must admit though that I enjoy the occasions when Nicholas has me ride with him on

Christmas Eve. It's good to get out of the house once in awhile."

"I would imagine so," I had to agree with her. "Although I dare say that there is enough going on around here to keep anyone from getting board too easily." Picking up the camera, I asked if I might snap some photo's to which she agreed with a nod of her head.

As I watched her through my lens, she reminded me of my own grandmother whom I had lost in previous years. I took several good shots then returned to my chair and retrieved my pad and pen. "I guess we should get started," I announced and waited for her to respond.

"So, what would you like to talk about first?" she asked point blank as she met my curious gaze. "We can discuss anything that your heart fancies."

A zillion questions shot through my mind, and I attempted to sort them into separate categories, each of which I fully intended to address in due time. But the question that was first, and foremost in my thoughts, spilled from my mouth before another had a chance to appear. "What is it like being Mrs. Santa Claus and living at the North Pole?"

"I count myself fortunate indeed to hold the position as wife of Santa Claus," Anna began with a deep sincerity that rang true in her voice. "Nary has a day passed when I don't count my blessings. I've often heard people ask if I grow weary of living so far away, on top of the world, and I can honestly say that I wouldn't change a moment of it."

My admiration for the woman grew with each word she uttered and I found myself envious of all she had. "Do you ever get lonely here?"

A warming smile creased her lips as she continued to stroke the soft fur on the purring kitten. "With a home so full of love, it's impossible to ever feel lonely. There is never a dull moment in this magical land where dreams are made to come true. Each day is a rush of activity as toys and gifts are being prepared for next years deliveries on Christmas Eve. Nicholas and I share a glorious life together and I can't imagine being anywhere but here where I belong."

"You mean that you and Santa never leave the North Pole for a vacation?" I was astounded at such a thought. "I love my home, but I also love my vacations, when I can ever find the time for one. Lately they've been few and far between."

"To be honest," Anna began in the softest of whispers, as though fearful of being overheard. "Santa and I do occasionally slip away on holiday."

"Now the truth is exposed," I said in jest. "So where do you go on vacation? What type of places could the two most famous people in the world go visit without being recognized?"

Santa has affection for Colorado, around the Rocky Mountains," she informed me much to my surprise for I had imagined something warmer, like Florida. "He likes to ski in Vale and rub elbows with those movie celebrities. Personally I enjoy the English countryside, a quaint cottage covered with flowers and ivy where piece and quiet prevail."

"But how do you keep people from recognizing you?" I questioned again for I couldn't imagine their being out in public without someone learning their identity. "You have to admit, Santa's beard gives him away."

Anna laughed openly and I relished in the sound of her voice. Something about her gave me a sense of peace inside, a feeling I had not known for quite some time. With a nod of her head, she agreed with my observation. "My dear, he gets recognized everywhere he goes, but no one actually believes it is him. Oh, people will point and say, 'there's a man who looks like Santa,' but they don't believe it to actually be him." A glimmer of sadness touched her bright eyes. "I'm afraid not many people do believe anymore," she stated in a soft tone.

"Children will always believe," I reminded her and instantly the sadness fled from her face. "There will always be skeptics in the world, people like I, who thought we had outgrown the notion of a jolly man in a red suite delivering presents on Christmas Eve. But as long as the children believe, as long as they keep Santa in their hearts, that's all that truly matters."

Reaching over, she gave my hand an affectionate squeeze. "How true, how true." The kitten, which had been sleeping in her lap, stood and gave a yawn as it stretched itself before leaping down to stroll from the room.

"The one thing I always wanted to know, as will thousands of children, is, how does Santa get down a chimney with a sack of toys, and what does he do when there is no chimney?" I couldn't wait to hear the answer to these questions for it was a mystery that had plagued me for years.

Anna gave me one of her delightful giggles which rang like music through the room. "Oh, my dear, Santa likes to keep a few things secret, but I will tell you this much, that he uses a little magic for it is a night of wondrous miracles."

"You evaded that one rather smoothly," I acknowledged with a giggle of my own and she laughed along with me. "Let's try this one," I continued. "No doubt that Rudolph is the most famous of reindeer, but does he always guide the sleigh as legend tells it?"

Lifting her gaze to the pictures on the wall, her vision focused on the deer with the bright red nose. "Rudolph is always in the lead, the other reindeer wouldn't have it any other way."

I found myself also studying the photo of Rudolph, transfixed by the glow illuminating from his nose. "Why does it shine so brightly?"

"When he was born, he was touched by Christmas magic," Anna replied as she returned her attention to me. "He is very precious to everyone here at Toy Land."

My childhood fascination with the reindeer returned to memory as I thought of several questions that had always puzzled me. Now I had the opportunity to discover their secrets. "What makes them fly, and can they fly any time they wish?"

"They only take flight on Christmas Eve," Anna said as she placed another log on the fire. "Many years ago, one of the elves discovered a special mixture of oats and corn, that when fed to the reindeer, would allow they to fly."

"How many reindeer live here at the North Pole?" I asked, my fascination growing by leaps and bounds. "Surely there are more to pull the sleigh in case one of the regular ones gets sick."

Leaning back in her rocker, Anna drew her shawl around her shoulders and began rocking slowly. "There are a lot of reindeer here, more than we can keep track of. The regular reindeer that pull Santa's sleigh never get sick. Like everyone here in

Toy Land, they are blessed with the touch of Christmas magic. Mother Nature and Father Time created a wonder land where time is irrelevant and health is eternal. A year for you is like a hundred years for us."

Just the thought of eternal life was mind boggling, yet it was something I was unsure if I could handle with the apparent ease that Anna did. "Imagine, never growing old," I thought aloud.

Anna chuckled softly and leaned over to touch my arm. "My dear, we grow old, it just takes us longer than most people. Good Heavens, do you think I was born looking like this?"

Her question caught me completely off guard, and the dumbfounded look on my face was apparent for it brought out another of her delightful giggles. "I was but a young girl when I met Nicholas. I lived in a land that you now call England, with my mother, Sarah, my father, Robert, three sisters and six brothers."

"It's hard to imagine you being anyone but Mrs. Clause," I said, still feeling somewhat stupefied by the revelation that Anna had a life before coming to the North Pole. "May I ask how you met Santa, and how you came to live here?"

Leaning back in her rocker, Anna sat silently for a moment, no doubt drawing on memories of a time long ago, now stored away as cherished treasures from the past. "A lot of curious people over the years have asked how I met Nicholas, as I prefer to call him. As the story has never been told, at least not correctly, I will oblige to relay it to you now."

I felt my heart quicken its pace with anticipation. I was about to learn one of the best kept secrets in the universe, and I was getting it straight from the source so there would be no mistakes. "Ready any time you are," I stated after flipping over the tape in the machine.

"As I stated before, I grew up on a farm in what you now call England. I continued to live there long after my father and mother passed on. I never married, for being the eldest child, I saw it my responsibility to care for the younger children until they were old enough to take flight from the nest. Once they were gone, I realized it was too late to start thinking of creating a new life for myself. I had willingly gave my future to my family, an I act I never once regretted for each grew up strong of mind, body and spirit."

"You must have loved them dearly to sacrifice so much," I said in awe of the woman for whom I was finding a new and deeper respect. "When did you finally meet Santa?"

Anna looked at the picture of herself and her husband that sat on the mantle. A loving smile caressed her lips as she thought back to a day so many years past. "I was nearing my fiftieth year, now living alone in the house where I was born. On Christmas Eve in the year 1198, after having my nightly cup of tea, I sat in my favorite chair beside the hearth and soon dozed. A strange sound awoke me from my slumber, the distinct sound of sleigh bells, and what seemed to be the hooves of reindeer as they landed upon my roof. At first I was startled, unsure of what to do, then a quiet calm covered me like the warmth of a favorite blanket."

"It was him? Wasn't it?" I couldn't wait for the answer. Goosebumps raced over my flesh, my heart was pounding anxiously. I was totally engrossed within the folds of the story, spellbound by each word she uttered.

Anna simply smiled and nodded. "I watched with wide eyes wonder as he appeared from down my chimney, his eyes instantly falling upon me. He was exactly as I imagined him to be. Broad of shoulder, beautiful white hair and a belly that told of too many snacks as he traveled the world. I spoke not a word as he approached and held out his hand for me to accept. Ever so gently he urged me to stand until I stood only inches from him. My hand was still within his gloved grasp when he spoke, the words rolling off his lips like sweet music."

Wide eyes, I leaned closer to Anna, wanting to make sure I didn't miss a single word she said. "What did he say?"

"Anna," "he called my name." "I have waited a long time for this treasured moment to arrive. I have watched you grow from a playful child to a woman whose heart knows no bounds. The love within you glows like a halo for all to see. You sacrificed your happiness for the sake of others, and in doing so, you have forever endeared yourself to me."

"Wow," was the only comment I could mutter.

"I was so stunned, I could nary speak," Anna said as she continued to gaze at the picture. "I stared at this mountain of a man and felt my heart and soul uniting with his own. I belonged with him; I knew this before he uttered another word."

"Wow," I babbled again. "How romantic. This is the kind of story novels are written about. So what happened next?"

"I have counted the days until it was time to come for you," Anna continued with her story. "He said, it is written in the stars, Anna that you are to be my wife. From this day forward, you will be known throughout the world as Mrs. Santa Claus."

Anna signed contently as she finally turned toward me. "Without any doubt, without any hesitation, I allowed Nicholas to escort me from the only home I had ever known. As I sat nestled beside him in the sleigh, I watched the lights of the world below flicker by as eight reindeer led the way to my new home. What awaited me, I had nary a clue, but I felt confident that whatever it was, it had been waiting for me all along. I was ready to begin my new life with the man I had loved since childhood, the man the world held in such high esteem. I have never regretted a single, glorious moment of it."

Realizing her story had concluded, I leaned back in my chair and let out a soft, content sigh. "That has got to be the most romantic thing I have ever heard in my life," I said with sincerity. I felt
extremely close to her for she had allowed me to touch a part of her life where no one else had ever been. I was privileged, and I had sense enough to realize it. "What about your wedding? Did it take place here at the North Pole? What was it like?"

Again, Anna smiled in fond remembrance as she thought back to that special day. "It was a fairytale come true," she said with a depth of love that knew no bounds. "Mother Nature was my bride's maid and Father Time delivered the vows. My gown was the most breathtaking creation imaginable. Cloth for the gown was woven from white angel hair, donated by the heavenly creations who blessed the union. The veil, and long train that flowed down my back were made of snowflakes, hand knitted by elves with great care and eminence love. My bouquet of roses was carved from ice, each pedal intricately detailed to perfection."

"Sounds glorious," I muttered as she paused but a brief moment. As she spoke, I could envision the wedding as though I was there as an honored guest. "Please continue."

"Nicholas wore his finest suite of red, the fur that trimmed it was white as the snow upon which we stood," she continued with the story. "A lane, lined with candy canes, led the way to the alter where I was escorted by Max, the senior elf here at Toy Land. All the reindeer stood around the alter to pay homage, and the Northern lights lit up the sky as if in celebration of the occasion."

"How marvelous," I commented and anxiously motioned for her to continue. "Please go on, it all sounds so romantic."

"Nicholas looked so proud as he stood waiting, his stature tall and regal, a bold smile caressing his lips. With each step I took, I could feel my heart swelling even more with the love that grew within it for him. As I stood proudly beside him, my hand held within his own, I knew as I gazed into his blue eyes that I was exactly where I belonged. When he removed the gold band from the pillow held by baby New Year, I trembled as he slid it onto my finger, forever sealing our fate." She sighed contently. "I've rattled on about myself long enough. I'm sure you have a lot of questions about Toy Land and Santa that would be much more interesting than hearing about my past."

"Are you kidding? Everyone will be fascinated to read about you," I informed her, for the information was intriguing. "You're one of the most famous, most beloved women in the world, yet so little is known about you. Anyone who reads this will be enchanted with what you've told me."

A light rap came to the door, followed by Penny entering with the tray of milk and cookies. "I thought you may enjoy some refreshments," she offered, placing the tray down upon a table near us. "Will there be anything else you might need?"

"No, and thank you for your thoughtfulness," Anna said with a smile to the young elf that she was obviously very fond of. "Just let us know when it's time for dinner."

With a nod of her head, Penny left the room, closing the door behind her. After a brief snack of cold milk and warm oatmeal cookies, I turned the recorder back on so we could continue with the interview. There were so many things I wanted to ask that it was hard to decide where to start.

"Once we finish here, I'll take you on a tour of Toy Land," Anna said much to my delight. It seemed she could read my mind for her next statement answered the question I so wanted to ask. "Who knows, we may even find Nicholas at a moment when he has time to sit and chat."

The broad smile that lit up my face was a dead give away that I more than approved.   I couldn't imagine having the opportunity to speak with Santa. Then again, I never thought I would be sitting in his home at the North Pole, sharing milk and cookies with Anna Claus. If my arm wasn't bruised from pinching myself so often, I would still think I was dreaming.

"How does Santa know which children have been naughty or nice?" I heard myself finally ask before taking another bite of the mouth-watering cookie.

"It's not as hard as one might suspect," Anna confessed with a chuckle.

"Of course parents, and teachers are a big help in letting us know how the children are doing, but it is the elves who keep a close check on everyone. And of course, Santa has his magical ways to check on certain ones throughout the year."

"Why doesn't anyone ever see Santa or the elves on Christmas Eve?" I questioned with a childish curiosity. "When I was little, I often waited up very late in hopes of catching a glimpse of him, but I never did."

Anna nodded her head knowingly. "I imagine many children have tried the same trick," she assumed. "Christmas Eve is a magical night for Santa and the elves. They are able to move at such great speed, it is almost impossible to detect them unless he allows it to happen."

"If Santa wants to please the children, then why are there some gifts that he doesn't bring? I'm talking about ones specifically asked for when the child writes to him?" I couldn't wait for the answer to this one, and knowing Anna, it would be a sound, and logical one.

Sitting aside her empty glass, she politely dabbed any remaining milk from her lips with the napkin before she spoke. "Often children ask for things that Santa knows their parents, or guardians would not approve of, so he must decline. Often, he also realizes that a particular gift is something special that the parents wish to purchase themselves. With so many children to please, he must often disappoint a few, and it breaks his heart to do so."

Before I had to utter a word, Anna leaned over and gently touched my cheek. As I gazed into her loving eyes, I found warmth and security within their glow. "I remember how upset he was when he had to disappoint you as a child. He truly wanted to bring you the ice skates, but your parents were fearful you would harm yourself. Nicholas never goes against a parent's wishes."

Her mention of the skates drew up a memory that I had buried long ago, near the same time I stopped believing in Santa. "I really wanted those skates," I heard myself confess. "I still remember how sad I was when I opened all the presents and they were not there. Christmas was never the same for me after that."

"I guess that happens quite often," Anna assumed. "One year Nicholas was so depressed because so many children had stopped believing that he threatened to cancel Christmas."

"Good Heavens," I gasped at such a thought. "A world without Christmas would be unimaginable. I realize that it's grown so commercial in today's society, but there are still people who believe."

Anna gave me a soft smile of reassurance and returned to the slow motion of her rocking. "Nicholas came to realize that. But as he always says, we should never forget what Christmas is truly about; the birth of our Lord and Savior, Jesus Christ. He is the true reason for the season."

"Amen," I said softly.

Slowly getting to her feet, Anna drew her shawl back up over her shoulder from where it had slipped. "I don't know about you, but I am growing weary of sitting. Come, let's take a stroll. We can continue to talk along the way."

Needing no further encouragement, I rose to follow her from the room. Not until I stood did I realize how tender my backside had become from so much time in the chair. Leaving the cozy room, void of any Christmas finery, was like leaving one world and entering another. Bright red poinsettias were abundant in every room, as were mountains of toys and workshops being tended to by hundreds of elves, each one working on a specific task.

"About how many toys are made here each day?" I asked, fascinated by the variety and quantity. Room after room was filled with everything from Yo-Yo's and Barbie dolls to Star Wars figures and remote control cars. Anything imaginable could be found stacked on a shelf someplace in Toy Land.

Pausing at the doorway to one of the workshops, we watched the elves rushing about in their duties. "It depends," Anna stated. "Toys that are complicated to make will naturally take longer so not as many can be made in a day. Simple toys like wooden rocking horses, building blocks and Lincoln Logs can be made in abundance. As you can tell by watching the elves, it's easy to see that each toy is made with love."

Her statement made me notice the faces of the elves, each one smiling or whistling a joyful tune as they worked. It was obvious they enjoyed their lives and I found myself a bit envious. "Does Santa need snow to make his deliveries?" I asked, once again following her down the hall. "I often wondered about the people who lived in places where it never snows.

"It would make the job much easier for him if there was snow, but no, Santa doesn't need it to make his deliveries." Anna paused at a set of large double door that were adorned with two of the most beautiful Christmas wreaths I had ever seen. "Personally, I love the snow. I enjoy seeing all the homes with their bright lights and decorations."

"I must admit, I enjoy it also," I confessed. "Where I'm from in Louisville, Kentucky, they have an event called 'Light up Louisville,' which I always attend. It's so beautiful when all the lights are turned on."

"I've seen it, and it is beautiful," Anna agreed with me. " There are several small towns the I enjoy seeing during the

Holidays. It lifts our hearts to see so many people getting into the Christmas spirit.

I was obviously surprised. "You go check out the Christmas lights?" I questioned.

Anna laughed at my obvious astonishment and I felt myself blush profusely. "I told you, Nicholas and I do get out occasionally," she reminded me. Without further ado, she pushed open the door to reveal a quaint country kitchen. A black, cast-iron cook stove sat in a brick lined alcove near the window. Copper kettles hung from the mantle which held colorful china. A decorative square rug covered the cobblestone floor and in the center of the rug was placed a small dining table with two chairs. A candle, with holly around the base, was the centerpiece on the white lace cloth that covered the table. Sitting beside the stove, a large tabby cat attempted to warm itself. The room was cozy and inviting to any guest which happened to enter.

"This is my private kitchen," Anna explained as we entered and closed the door. "Please have a seat and I'll fix us something warm to drink."

Placing myself in the chair nearest the warm stove, I watched as Anna prepared a cup of coffee for me and a cup of apple cinnamon tea for her. "Is this where you and Santa eat your meals?"

"Occasionally, when we feel the need to spend some quality time together," Anna explained as she seated herself in the other chair. "I like to come here and work on recipes, experiment with a few on occasions. I call it my little corner of the world."

"I can see why, I love it in here," I agreed. "I'd love to have a kitchen like this. When I get back home, I may work on that. I've wanted to remodel my kitchen and now I know what I want to do with it."

"I'm glad you like it," Anna said, obviously pleased that I liked the room. "Nicholas had it built and decorated like the kitchen in the home where I grew up. Would you believe that this is the actual stove my mother had?"

Instantly my eyes locked on the shiny black cast iron stove and I stared with fascination. "Now that is really an antique," I commented. "I must say, it's held up well over the years."

Anna touched it with the affection one would bestow upon a child. "It's my most treasured possession," she quickly looked at me and winked. "Next to Nicholas, of course."

"Oh, of course," I agreed and chuckled at her jest. "May I ask if you have any children?" I turned on the recorder and waited for the answer.

Without turning around, Anna continued with her task. "I have many children," she answered. "All the children of the world." She turned slowly to face me, a touch of sadness in her normally bright eyes. "Nicholas and I never had any children of our own. I guess it wasn't meant to be."

I hated to hear the sorrow in her voice and wished I had never asked the question that obviously gave her pain. "Sorry, I didn't mean to pry," I apologized. "It must be hard not having any of your family around. Do you know if there are any ancestors still living in England?"

Instantly her eyes returned to their bright twinkle. "Many of them still live there, and I try to visit when I can."

Her statement surprised me. "Do they know who you really are? That you're married to Santa?"

Returning to the table, Anna placed my cup before me then sat in the empty chair. "Only a very few know the truth. The others simply know me as a distant relative."

"Very distant," I said with a chuckle. "What about Santa? Does he still have any relatives somewhere in the world?"

"I'm afraid he had no blood relatives still living," Anna replied as she stirred the tea in her cup, its aroma enticing my senses. "Santa considers everyone around the world his family. That is why he takes such great joy in delivering the gifts each Christmas Eve."

"Since you have no children, what happens if, or when, Santa decides it is time to retire. Surely he can't do this forever."

Anna sipped her tea and thought for a moment. "I guess that day will eventually come, Nicholas and I have discussed it at great lengths." She said. "When it is time, Santa will choose a replacement, someone from your world who is worthy of wearing the red suite."

I was stunned, to say the least. "Replace Santa….I can't imagine it."

Anna smiled. "It will be difficult, but Father Time keeps a list of worthy souls, one of which would be selected if that day ever comes. But don't worry about such things," she gave my hand a reassuring pat. "Nicholas is still a spry man and he will carry on for many years to come."

"Why is it that he only comes once a year?" I sipped my coffee to detect a pinch of nutmeg and found it refreshing.

Anna gave me one of her delightful giggles as she leaned back in her chair. "Good Heavens, that's all he has time for. With so many stops to make, and so many people to care for, it takes a full year to get ready for the next delivery date."

"Do you know how the tradition of hanging stockings on the mantle came to be?" I took another sip and waited for her reply.

"The story goes," she began to explain. "there was a father who had daughters of marrying age, but he could not afford a dowry for them. St. Nicholas heard of the man's troubles and secretly dropped three bags of coins down the chimney. They landed in the girl's stockings which they had placed on the hearth to dry. Once word spread of the miracle, the tradition began."

"Fascinating," I commented after another sip of the delicious coffee. When Anna offered a selection of cookies and candies, I found myself nibbling shamelessly.

"One of my favorite traditions is the burning of the Yule log," Anna said between bites of a walnut cookie. "It's an ancient tradition really. To burn it during winter solstice, symbolized the coming of warm, sunny days. It was believed to bring protection and good luck to those who burned the log. Some believed it symbolized the light of heaven."

"Does it have to be a certain type of wood?" I had no idea why I asked, for to me, wood is wood.

With a nod of her head, Anna went on to explain. "It is usually oak. Often a piece of kindling is removed before lighting the log, and put safely away. The following year, the new log is started with the piece to symbolize continuity."

Pausing the interview for a moment, I flipped over the tape in the recorder and turned it on. "You have such an interesting life, Anna. I know you have Santa, but don't you ever get lonely for female companionship? I don't mean the elves, but someone your own size?"

Anna looked somewhat surprised, then laughed softly. "I keep forgetting that you don't know how things work here at the

North Pole. I have plenty of female friends; they visit from all over the world."

"For real?" I was no doubt astounded and it apparently showed on my face for Anna again giggled that delightful giggle. "You mean people like me come to the North Pole to visit you and Santa?"

"Of course dear." Anna sipped her tea then continued. "Folks are always dropping by for a visit, folks just like you."

"Like who?" I was anxious to get the names of those who called the Claus's friends.

"It wouldn't be right to namedrop," Anna stated. "All I will say is this; they are folks who never, ever stopped believing in Santa. As a reward for their lifelong belief, we often have them hear as guest. You would be surprised at how many adults still believe in Santa Claus."

"Well knock me over with a feather," I mumbled, still surprised by the confession. It was hard to fathom any adult still believing in Santa, then again, I was now a believer, and I had to be since I was sitting in the kitchen of his home. "Readers will be fascinated to hear about this. I must say, you've told me a lot of things that the world will find interesting."

Anna flashed me one of her warmest smiles. "I hope so my dear, that is why I wanted to do this interview. I thought it time the world knew the truth."

"Maybe when the book is published, you can come to some book signing with me," I said, actually in jest for I never dreamed of what her reply would be.

"I'd love to," Anna answered. "Let me know when and where." Standing, she took our empty cups and placed them in the sink. "Come now, let's finish the tour. Care to see the reindeer?"

In a flash, I was on my feet and racing out of the room after her. I was actually going to see the famous reindeer, maybe even have the chance to touch one. My heart was racing like a runaway train and I couldn't believe how excited I was. I followed Anna so closely that it was a wonder I didn't trip over her feet. Entering an extremely large stable area that was attached to the main house by a long hall, I instantly smelled the aroma of animal musk. Even before we reached the stalls, I heard the sound of deer munching on hay, and the occasional rake of antlers against the side of the stall. My heart rate increased with each step I took.

Rounding the corner I came to an abrupt halt, the air catching in my throat to emit a loud gasp. "Oh my Heavens, is that what I think it is?"

Anna smiled and turned her attention to the large, bright red sleigh resting in an alcove. "Yes, it's Santa's sleigh. Would you like to sit in it?"

My heart fell to the bottom of my boots. "You mean I can really climb in? It would be all right?" I felt like a child who just received the greatest gift of all time.

"I don't believe Nicholas would mind," Anna assured me with a warm smile. Taking my hand, she escorted me toward the sleigh and held my equipment as I eagerly slipped into the driver's compartment, sinking into the plush velvet covered seat.

"I can't believe I'm actually doing this." My hands caressed each curve and contour of the bright red sleigh with its velvet seats. My heart raced with childish excitement as I imagined myself holding the reins to eight magical reindeer as we sailed through the night sky.

"Smile," Anna called out. I looked up as the flash on my camera exploded, illuminating the room in its bright light. "Thought you might like a picture for a souvenir."

"Thank you," I said while reluctantly stepping out of the sleigh. I would have loved to stay longer, but there were more wondrous sights to see, and I was unsure of how much time I had left in Toy Land. "May I see the reindeer now?"

"Most certainly," Anna replied, and motioned for me to follow. "They love having company stop by for a visit. Gives them a chance to show off a bit."

With eager steps, I followed Anna through the open door into the long row of stalls. One by one, antlered heads began to appear from over the stall doors as each reindeer curiously looked at the stranger invading their home. Dasher gave me a snort of annoyance for interrupting his lunch, and Prancer shook his massive antler to make certain I didn't miss him in passing. Each reindeer was eager for a gentle pat on the nose and my words of praise for their beauty. Like children, each vied for my attention as we strolled past. I was amazed at how distinctive each was, in personality, and in appearance.

Dasher was the most distinguishable of the group with his massive antlers. Dancer had friendly eyes and Prancer wore a white spot just over his right eye. Vixen had a thin white strip of hair racing down the middle of his face while Comet had a bold star on his forehead. Cupid carried a white snip of hair on his nose and Donner had no white on his face at all. Blitzen was the most colorful of the group for not only did he have a bold star on his forehead, he also had a narrow blaze and his two hind legs were white to the knees. But it was the last stall that held the reindeer I was most anxious to see. Rudolph the red nose reindeer.

Before I arrived at the stall, I saw the soft red glow coming from within. My heart sped up with each eager step I took. Then I saw him and my heart skipped a beat as it lodged within my throat. There he stood, in all his magical glory, Rudolph with his nose so bright.

"I can't believe it's actually him," I rambled like an awe struck child. "He's more magnificent that I imagined."

"He's quite the character," Anna chuckled as she gave Rudolph an affectionate pat on the neck. "He is very special to all of us here at Toy Land. I guess you know the story of how he helped save Christmas by lighting the way through the blinding snow with his shinning nose."

"I doubt if there is anyone in the world who doesn't know the story," I answered as Rudolph nuzzled by pockets to see if they contained any treats. "It's one of the most famous tales of all time."

"Rudolph, be nice," Anna scolded the rambunctious deer as he stomped his hoof impatiently when I did not make a treat appear for his pleasure. "I'm afraid he has a sweet tooth, he loves peppermint candy."

"Wish I had some for him." Digging deep within my jacket pocket, I managed to locate a single M&M candy which he eagerly accepted. "Sorry, but that's all I have."

"We should be heading back to the main house," Anna suggested as she took my arm to get me started. "It's just about supper time, and the chef elves get upset when anyone is late. Besides, I'm getting a bit hungry myself."

I had to admit that the slight rumble in my stomach had grown louder the last few minutes. "A meal does sound good," I agreed with her. Before leaving the stables, I cast a glance back over my shoulder for one last peek at the reindeer. It was definitely a memory that would stay with me for eternity.

Before we even arrived at the dinning hall, I could smell the delicious aromas drifting out to tease our senses. The tantalizing smells only made my stomach growl louder and Anna chuckled and said I sounded like a bear. As the door opened, and we entered, I froze in my tracks. Never in my wildest dreams could I have imagined the sight that met me. Elves, in all shapes and sizes, seated in chairs around the many tables that filled the massive room. It sounded like the chatter of hundreds of children as the elves held conversations with others around them.

"Good Heavens, there sure is a lot of them," I said in awe of the wondrous sight. "Looks like a million or more."

Anna again offered her delightful giggle as she ushered me to a smaller, round table nestled near the fireplace. "Not near that many, my dear," she replied. "Just a few thousand workers and their families."

I could not conceive someone actually cooking for that many and I would never have believed it if I had not seen it for myself. As we seated ourselves, I noticed only three place settings. "We don't eat with the elves?"

"Normally we do, but since we have a guest, the elves set this table us for us," Anna explained as she laid the white napkin across her lap.

When all at once the chatter stopped, and silence filled the room, I wondered what was happening as each and every elf stood, their eyes focused on the door. I Amazed I watched the mountain of a man who entered the room. His long white beard was combed to perfection and hung down midway of his broad chest. His eyes twinkled with childish delight as he approached our table and tenderly took Anna's hand, placing a kiss upon it.

"My dear, you look enchanting," He spoke in a deep tone, yet there was a light jolliness to the sound. "But then, you always do."

I knew him instantly, although he did not wear his traditional red suite, instead opting for a red and black flannel shirt and black trousers. No matter what he wore, there was no denying the fact that Santa himself had entered the room. I to awe-struck to move.

Anna blushed like a schoolgirl and playfully tapped his arm. "You're such a tease Nicholas. Now behave yourself, we have company."

Instantly his attention was focused upon me. I didn't know what to do, or what to say. Did I bow in his presence? Did I remain silent until he acknowledged my presence? I was so nervous at meeting him, I could only sit there, mouth open like a fool, and stare wide eyed at the most beloved man in the world.

"So, you're the writer that Anna has been so excited about," Santa said, extending his hand for me to take. "Pleased to meet you Mrs. Marr, I have heard a lot about you."

"I've heard a lot about you also," I said, and instantly felt like a fool for everyone knew about Santa. I rolled my eyes at my stupidity. "I'm very pleased to meet you, sir," I managed to babble as I accepted his hand in greeting.

Taking his chair between us, Santa smiled and leaned back comfortably. "I hope you've enjoyed your visit so far. I'm sure Anna has been the perfect host, as she always is."

"Oh yes, Anna has been wonderful. I must say, there are no words that can adequately describe the feeling I have inside, or what this experience has meant to me. I feel very honored." I accepted the cup of coffee being served by a waiter elf and waited for him to finish before I continued. "I think my biggest thrill was seeing the reindeer. They are so beautiful."

Santa nodded his head in agreement. "Yes, the boys are very special to everyone here. Without them, there could be no Christmas deliveries. Normally they run free around the North Pole, but we bring them in about a week before Christmas to feed extra rations. We want them strong and healthy for their flight. Most people don't realize how strenuous the trip is for them."

"Takes nearly a month for them to rest up afterwards," Anna added to the conversation then chuckled softly. "It takes Nicholas about as long."

Santa huffed as though insulted by her statement. He said not a word as the elves carried our plates to the table, each filled with mouth-watering delights.

Everything looked so scrumptious; I didn't know where to start. Baked whitefish, macaroni and cheese and a baked potato spiced to taste with sour cream, chives and bacon bits. Each tasty morsel I consumed was a delight to my taste buds. It was so delicious, I happily accepted seconds when offered. I may not have done so if I'd know what was planned for desert. We had our choice of angel food cake, smothered with strawberries and whip-cream. Banana pudding, pumpkin or apple pie and any type of cookie imaginable. I'm ashamed to admit I had a taste of each, and was forced to open the button of my jeans to accommodate my bulging stomach.

"I'm about to explode," I groaned in misery as we left the table. "I can't believe I made such a pig of myself, but it was all so scrumptious."

Santa laughed his famous Ho, Ho, Ho, and rubbed his round belly. "Now you can see why I stay so plump in the middle."

Anna laughed happily, also touching her belly. "I must admit the same for me. The elves are such good cooks; it's hard to push the plate away."

"I assume Anna has already shown you around Toy Land. But, would you care for a tour of North Pole City?" Santa asked while leading us down a long hallway. "I imagine there are some sights that may interest you."

"You bet I would," was my immediate comeback. I felt immensely privileged. I was being taken on a tour that few had ever seen, and I had Santa Claus himself for a tour guide.

Leaving the warmth of Toy Land, we climbed into a sleigh being pulled by two reindeer with Santa at the reins. Anna and I sat nestled cozy beneath warm blankets as the sleigh glided over the packed snow. Our first stop was the elf school where youngsters learned their ABC's. Next we stopped at the large Polar Post Office where millions of letters arrived daily from children around the world, each note filled with Christmas wishes. Another stop found us in the building that housed the naughty and nice list. Elves worked around the clock, supervising children around the world, and keeping reports of their behavior on computers. We checked out the weather station, where elves kept a close watch on conditions for Santa's Christmas Eve ride, then we made quick stops at the radio and the television station. We drove down lanes lined with beautifully decorated homes where some of the elves lived, and paused to watch couples skating on the frozen pond.

I was cold, yet I hated for the tour to end. Everything I had seen was so magical and wondrous that I never wanted to leave. I felt a peace and comfort that I had never experienced before and it left me feeling warm inside. As we returned to the main house and shed our heavy coats and gloves, we were met by elves with hot cups of cocoa which really hit the spot. Seating ourselves beside the hearth where a roaring fire danced to soft Christmas music playing from the radio, I found my eyes growing heavy. I tried to concentrate on the stories being told and the questions asked of me, but my mind kept drifting off to slumber.

"Good Heaven, Nicholas, we've worn the child out with all our rattling," Anna stated as she stood to remove the half empty cup from my hand before I spilled it. "I think it's time we all retire for the night. After all, you need your rest, considering what tomorrow is."

"Tomorrow?" I questioned as I drug myself to my feet. "What about tomorrow? Did I miss something?"

"Tomorrow is Christmas Eve," Santa said with a chuckle. "Did you forget about it?"

Confused, I looked from one to another, waiting for an explanation. "But it can't be Christmas Eve, I came here a month before Christmas to do the interview. I've only been here a day. Someone has their calendar messed up."

Both Santa and Anna chuckled with delight. "Time is irrelevant here my dear, remember? I told you that at the beginning," Anna explained. "A month for you is but a mere day to us."

I held up my hand to prevent her from continuing. "Please, don't explain for I'm much to tired. When I get like this, I will forget what you told me by morning." I picked up my recorder and camera. "If you don't mind, I'd like to spend some time tomorrow typing on the story. I have plenty of information on the recorder to start with."

Santa smiled. "What ever you wish, is fine with us."

Anna took my arm to escort me from the room. "Come along dear, I'll show you back to your room. It's easy to become lost if you don't know your way around."

Giving Santa a wave good-by, I followed Anna from the room, anxious to lay my head on a soft pillow and catch some much needed sleep. If tomorrow was Christmas Eve as they said, then I wanted to be rested and ready to jump in and help if needed. The thought excited me. Imagine, helping load the sleigh with toys for Santa to deliver, and being there to watch him take flight. It was a thrilling image, one I looked forward to. It would be something I could one day tell my children and grandchildren, how I helped Santa prepare for his magical night.

Nestled beneath warm blankets, I slept like a baby, so much so that I never heard nary a sound throughout the night. As the sun filtered in through my window, I stretched and yawned which was my usual routine in the morning. As my eyes adjusted to the light, my serenity quickly turned to confusion. I sat bolt upright and looked around the room, my confusion mounting as I slid from the bed, in my own home. Dumbfounded was to kind a word to express my state of mind. I stood in the center of the room, continuing to look around as though waiting for some explanation to arrive. Sitting on the edge of the bed, I tried to figure out what had happened, but there was no logical answer. I was frightened and confused.

When I spotted the small recorder sitting on my desk beside the camera, I raced to it. Snatching it up, I pushed the play button only to hear dead silence. My confusion deepened. I checked the camera to discover it empty as well. I was on the verge of thinking I had lost my mind when I noticed the large manila envelope. Picking it up, I carefully slid the manuscript from within it. My heart skipped a beat when I read the titled printed boldly across the first page. It said, 'Anna Clause, the Woman Behind the Legend. Written by: Karen Marr.'

I raced to the kitchen where over a cup of coffee, I read the entire manuscript in record breaking time. It was good. But when had I written it? Had I experienced nothing more than a dream? It couldn't have been, it was far too real to be some figment of my imagination. I met Santa and Anna Claus, I saw the elves, and I touched the reindeer and sat in the sleigh. I know I did. I just know it.

When I looked at the front page again, I noticed the date. My confusion mounted. How could I have been gone a month? And when had I written this manuscript? I don't remember typing a single word of it, yet here is was, held within my trembling grasp.

"My editor," I finally found the words to speak, but even they sounded rattled due to my confusion. "I know Peggy will remember sending me to the North Pole to do the story."

Racing back to my bedroom, I dressed with lightning speed and fled from my apartment, barely remembering to snatch up my purse on the way out. Hailing a cab, I scrambled inside and barked directions to the driver. As we made our way through traffic, my mind worked overtime, attempting to sort out all that had happened.

Handing the driver his fair, I hurried into the building as though my feet had sprouted wings. Not waiting for the receptionist to announce me, I burst through the door into Peggy's office. Before I had time to utter a word, she stood and flashed me a broad smile.

"I was just about to call you," she announced, moving around the chair to greet me. "Your book just hit number one on the best sellers list."

If I had been confused before, it was even worse now. "Book? What book?" I babbled like a raving lunatic.

"Why, your Mrs. Claus book. What else would I be referring to? We got it out just at the right time during the Christmas season. It was a tight rush, but we made it." Peggy watched me, and from her expression, I could tell she was totally confused.

My legs felt like Jell-O as I dropped heavily into the plush leather chair. "I've lost my mind," I rambled." Hoping for an explanation, I looked at Peggy for answers. "Something has happened to me, Peggy. I don't remember writing the book."

Seating herself in a chair beside me, Peggy patted my hand in a motherly fashion and smiled softly. "It's a wonder you're sane at all the way you crammed to get this book done for Christmas. You locked yourself away in your apartment for a month, refusing calls and never venturing outside. I appreciate dedication, but my dear, you almost went too far."

"I've been home for a month?" My mind made yet another attempt to remember a tiny fragment of the past weeks, but all I could visualize was my North Pole trip. "I've definitely been working to hard," I assumed aloud. From the way she talked, it was obvious that Peggy had no idea of what I was rattled about. I wanted to explain everything I had seen to her, but I was fearful she would think me totally insane. "That's the only explanation I can come up with. I got so involved in the story, I lost touch with reality. Simple as that." My explanation made sense yet I felt no better.

"Do you remember sending me to the North Pole for this story?" I had to ask.

"North Pole, what on earth are you talking about?" Peggy questioned as she watched me with concern. I think you need a long vacation."

"A vacation?" I mumbled. "Just what I need, another vacation." Slowly getting to my feet, I walked toward the door. "I'll call you later to let you know what I'm doing."

Before she could respond, I closed the door between us. Back out on the street, I decided to walk the four blocks back to my apartment. Maybe the cold December air would help clear my flustered mind. The more I thought, the more confused I became. Had I really been at the North Pole? Had I talked with Santa and Anna Claus? How could it be? Anna had said that it was the day before Christmas Eve, that was the last I remember. Now I was back in New York, the day before Christmas with a new book on the shelves. Oh, it was all to confusing.

Passing the local bookstore, I stopped abruptly when my eyes locked upon the book in the display window. It was Mrs. Claus, the book I could not remember writing. People were snatching them up and scurrying to the counter to pay for their selection. With a confused shake of my head, I continued on down the sidewalk. With each step I took came the reality that I may never know what actually happened. Maybe it was better for my sanity if I never did.

Returning to my apartment, I turned on the lights to the Christmas tree, and paused to marvel at its beauty. Over the past years, I had come to look at the tree as a simple Christmas decoration, quite often a nuance when it came time to take it down. Now, as I gazed upon its splendor, I marveled at the magic it symbolized.

Fixing myself a sandwich, I flopped down comfortably on the sofa to watch my collection of Christmas classics, starting with, 'It's A Wonderful Life.' One holiday movie followed another until the clock on the wall said it was time to retire. Snuggled beneath warm blankets, I drifted off to a place where reindeer could fly, elves made toys, and a jolly man in a red suite laughed his famous ho, ho, ho.

When my eyes fluttered open at the dawn of a new day, I sat up to yawn and stretch. Suddenly I remembered what day it was and scurried into the living room to open the stack of gifts received from family and friends. I marveled at each one, and made a mental note to send everyone a thank you card for their thoughtfulness. I was just about to stand when a package hidden near the back of the tree, caught my eye. Dragging it out, I searched in vain for a name tag, and my curiosity mounted as I examined the medium size package with its huge bow and bright red wrappings.

Removing the paper, I anxiously slid off the lid and stared in surprise at the beautiful set of ice skates. Removing the Christmas card from inside, I felt my heart skip a beat as I read the cherished words. "Karen, here are the skates you asked for so long ago. I'm sure your parents would not objections now to you having them. We enjoyed your book, and maybe someday you will autograph it for us. Until we see you again, Santa and Anna Claus."

I stared at the card through moist eyes until all the words ran together amid my flow of tears. Although I had nary a clue as to what had happened to me over the past month, or how it had taken place, at least now I knew that I wasn't insane. Maybe one day, if I was fortunate enough, I would return to the magical land of the North Pole, where once again I would sip coffee with Anna in her cozy kitchen, watch elves scurry about, busy with their toy making, and again visit all the reindeer as they munched hay in their stalls.

I was honored to have seen such wondrous sights, and to have met Anna and her husband, Nicholas. Until that day comes, I will continue on with my life, and forever cherish the special memories I was given by the Queen of the frozen North and the most beloved man in the world, Santa Claus. As he is so fond of saying, "Merry Christmas to All, and To All a Good Night."

[THE END]

Jolene Giordano & Linda Dockery

Who's Who in America 2004

Who's Who of American Writers 2004

Who's Who of American Women 2004